W9-BJL-401

CAMILA
THE SINGING STAR

written by ALICIA SALAZAR

illustrated by THAIS DAMIÃO

PICTURE WINDOW BOOKS
a capstone imprint

Published by Picture Window Books, an imprint of Capstone
1710 Roe Crest Drive, North Mankato, Minnesota 56003
capstonepub.com

Library of Congress Cataloging-in-Publication Data
Names: Salazar, Alicia, 1973- author. | Damião, Thais, illustrator. | Salazar,
Alicia, 1973- Camila the star.
Title: Camila the singing star / by Alicia Salazar ; illustrated by Thais Damiao.
Description: North Mankato, Minnesota : Picture Window Books, an imprint
of Capstone, [2022] | Series: Camila the star | Audience: Ages 5-7. | Audience:
Grades K-1. | Summary: Camila has entered a singing competition, and she
knows that she wants to sing her family's favorite song. When it comes to
actually competing, though, Camila is very nervous about the size of the
audience and being in the spotlight. But Camila knows her family is there and
that she can use that knowledge to overcome her stage fright. Includes artistic
activity.
Identifiers: LCCN 2021033307 (print) | LCCN 2021033308 (ebook) | ISBN
9781663958709 (hardcover) | ISBN 9781666331684 (paperback) | ISBN
9781666331691 (pdf)
Subjects: LCSH: Hispanic American girls—Juvenile fiction. | Singing—
Juvenile fiction. | Contests—Juvenile fiction. | Stage fright—Juvenile fiction.
| Self-confidence—Juvenile fiction. | CYAC: Hispanic Americans—Fiction.
| Singing—Fiction. | Contests—Fiction. | Stage fright—Fiction. | Self-
confidence—Fiction. | Hispanic Americans—Fiction. | LCGFT: Picture books.
Classification: LCC PZ7.1.S2483 Car 2022 (print) | LCC PZ7.1.S2483 (ebook) |
DDC [E]—dc23
LC record available at https://lccn.loc.gov/2021033307
LC ebook record available at https://lccn.loc.gov/2021033308

Designer: Hilary Wacholz

Printed and bound in the USA. PO4608

TABLE OF CONTENTS

Meet Camila and Her Family

Papá

Mamá

Ana, age 14

Andres, age 10

Camila, age 7

Spanish Glossary

abuela (ah-BWEH-lah)—grandmother

Aquellos ojos verdes (ah-KEH-yohs OH-hohs VEHR-dehs)—song lyrics meaning, "Those green eyes"

Eres mi orgullo (EH-res MEE or-GOO-yoh)—You are my pride

gordita (gor-DEE-ta)—a small patty made from cornmeal

masa (MAH-sa)—dough

Serenos como un lago (seh-REH-nos KOH-moh OON LAH-goh)—song lyrics meaning, "Calm like a lake"

Si puedo (SEE PUE-eh-do)—I can

Chapter 1
THOSE GREEN EYES

Camila yawned as she walked into the kitchen on Sunday morning.

Her **abuela** was kneading the **masa** for **gorditas**. She was singing her favorite song.

Camila loved when Abuela sang. Her voice was like a warm blanket.

Camila ran to Abuela and gave her a big hug. Then she hummed along and patted the **masa** into balls.

Mamá joined them in the kitchen. "**Aquellos ojos verdes** . . . ," she sang.

She patted the balls into circles and put them on the griddle.

Ana, Andres, and Papá heard the singing. They came to see what was happening.

"**Serenos como un lago . . . ,**" the three of them joined in. They began setting the table.

After the last note, they all laughed and patted each other on the back.

"The best music is what love sounds like," said Abuela.

The family sat down to eat.

"Speaking of music," said Andres, "are you excited for the singing contest next week, Camila?"

"Yes!" Camila said. "I know just the song to sing."

Chapter 2

ALL ALONE

Camila practiced her song every day that week. Ana and Andres listened to her sing.

"Not so high," said Ana.

"Not so low," said Andres.

Camila kept working. She would be ready for the contest.

The day of the contest, Camila put on her most glittery dress.

"I look like a star," she thought.

But she worried about losing her voice . . . or forgetting the words . . . or hitting a sour note.

"Just imagine that your family are the only people watching," said Mamá. "And sing from your heart."

"**Eres mi orgullo**," said Papá.

"I haven't won yet," said Camila.

"We are proud of you no matter what," said Papá. He gave her a big hug.

"We will be there cheering for you," said Papá.

"Good luck," said Andres. He gave her a fist bump.

"Break a leg," said Ana. She gave her a kiss on the cheek.

Mamá dropped Camila off backstage and went to find a program.

Camila took a peek at the stage. There were so many lights.

She looked at all the chairs. They would soon be filled with fans.

Camila felt nervous. "I'll be okay if my family is here," she thought.

She closed her eyes.

"Just imagine they are the only ones watching," Camila told herself.

"There is nothing to worry about," she thought. "They will be here."

Chapter 3
A WINNER

"Our next young singer is Camila Maria Flores Ortiz," said the host. "Come on out, Camila!"

Camila stepped onto the stage.

She squinted, trying to see her family. She only saw Mamá just offstage.

Suddenly, she was worried again. What if she forgot the words . . . or lost her voice . . . or sang off-key?

Mamá gave her a thumbs up.

Camila stepped on her mark on the stage. She looked out into the crowd again.

There were so many people, but she couldn't find her family.

Camila felt frozen. Her chest was heavy.

She blinked. When she
opened her eyes, she saw signs
held up by fans she didn't know
she had.

"**Si puedo**," Camila thought.
"I can do my best."

She took a deep breath. She began singing with all her heart. **"Aquellos ojos verdes . . ."**

She imagined her family singing along. She felt wrapped in a warm blanket.

When the song was over, she looked out at the crowd again.

This time she saw her family.
There were Papá, Abuela, Ana,
and Andres cheering her on.
     She and Mamá did a happy
dance as she walked offstage.

"You were a star tonight," said Mamá.

"I haven't won yet," said Camila.

"But you did it, all by yourself," said Mamá.

"I felt like I was wrapped in a warm blanket," said Camila. "The best music doesn't just sound like love, it *feels* like love too."

Make a Concert Poster

Singers and bands hang up posters to tell people about their upcoming shows. Pretend you are a singing star, and make a concert poster. Here are some tips on making a great concert poster:

WHAT YOU NEED
- paper
- markers or something else to write and draw with
- photos or other items you may want to glue onto your poster (optional)
- glue (optional)

Think about the mood your poster should have. How does your music make people feel? Your poster should match those feelings. For pop music, you might use bright colors. For love songs, you might use hearts on your poster.

Make your poster stand out. Draw attention to the poster. Big, clear words can get people's attention. A cool picture or photo can make people take a closer look. Bright colors make people stop.

Share important information on your poster.

Make sure to include:

- who is giving the concert

- where the concert is

- when the concert is, including date and time

Glossary

backstage (BAK-stayj)—the area behind the stage of a theater

glittery (GLIT-uh-ree)—decorated with tiny pieces of sparkling material

griddle (GRID-uhl)—a flat surface or pan on which food is cooked

nervous (NUR-vuhs)—feeling worried or anxious

note (NOHT)—a musical sound

offstage (AWF-stayj)—off or away from the stage, outside of the view of the audience

program (PROH-gram)—a written list describing what will be presented at a show or concert

squint (SKWINT)—to look with eyes partly closed

Think About the Story

1. Abuela says the best music sounds like love. Why do you think she said that? What do you think that means?

2. What song did Camila sing? How do you know?

3. Imagining her family singing along with her made Camila feel like she was wrapped in a warm blanket. What gives you that feeling?

4. Imagine you were in a singing contest. How would you feel? Compare that to Camila's feelings in the book.

About the Author

Alicia Salazar is a Mexican American children's book author who has written for blogs, magazines, and educational publishers. She was also once an elementary school teacher and a marine biologist. She currently lives in the suburbs of Houston, Texas, but is a city girl at heart. When Alicia is not dreaming up new adventures to experience, she is turning her adventures into stories for kids.

About the Illustrator

Thais Damião is a Brazilian illustrator and graphic designer. Born and raised in a small city in Rio de Janeiro State, Brazil, she spent her childhood playing with her brother and cousins and drawing all the time. Her illustrations are dedicated to children and inspired by nature and friendship. Thais currently lives in California.